For Jude and Maisie, with love
J. R.

For Joy, Lance, Mione, and George, with love
T. B.

This edition published by Parragon Books Ltd in 2014 and distributed by

Parragon Inc.
440 Park Avenue South, 13th Floor
New York, NY 10016
www.parragon.com

Published by arrangement with Gullane Children's Books

Text © Julia Rawlinson 2013
Illustrations © Tiphanie Beeke 2013

ISBN 978-1-4723-3765-8

Printed in China

Fletcher's Big Show

Julia Rawlinson

Tiphanie Beeke

Bath • New York • Singapore • Hong Kong • Cologne • Delhi
Melbourne • Amsterdam • Johannesburg • Shenzhen

It was a beautiful sun-baked day, and the woods were
sleepy in the heat. Fletcher lay in the shade of a tree,
watching sunlight dancing on the leaves.

He could hear birds singing in the trees, frogs
croaking in the pond, crickets chirping in the grass, and ...

... a sad, snuffling sound. Fletcher looked around and there, among the ferns, was a very small rabbit.

"What's wrong?" asked Fletcher.

"I'm useless," sniffed the rabbit. "The birds can sing, the frogs can croak, the crickets can chirp—and I can't do anything."

"Maybe you can learn," said Fletcher. "Let's ask the birds."

The birds were chirruping high in the sun-dappled branches.
Fletcher called up to ask them to teach Rabbit to sing.

"Open your beak and trill," said the birds.

"But I don't have a beak," said Rabbit.

"Try opening your mouth," said Fletcher, but no
trill came out.

"*Frogs* don't have beaks," said Fletcher.
"I'm sure they will help."

The frogs were croaking in their pond,
deep in a shady glade.
  Fletcher crouched down and asked
them to teach Rabbit to croak.

"Puff out your throat,"
said the frogs, but Rabbit's
throat wouldn't puff.

"Try puffing out your cheeks,"
said Fletcher, but that wasn't
noisy enough.

"*Crickets* don't have beaks
or puffy throats," said Fletcher.
"Don't give up."

Fletcher and Rabbit hurried from the shady woods into the buttercup meadow where the crickets were chirping in the sun.

"Rub your wings together," said the crickets.

"But I don't have any wings," said Rabbit.

"Try rubbing your arms," said Fletcher, but that didn't work.

"It's no good," sighed Rabbit. "I'm too fluffy to chirp."

Fletcher and Rabbit flopped down
in the cool shade of a tree.
"I'm sorry I couldn't help,"
said Fletcher, gazing up at the leaves.
They lay quietly side by side,
watching the patterns of dark
and light until their eyes began to
close, and they fell fast asleep.

While they slept, the sun moved slowly through the
cloudless sky. Shadows stretched silently across the grassy ground.
Little by little, a golden shaft of sunlight crept over them ...

… so when he awoke, Fletcher felt as though he was spotlighted on a stage.

"That's it!" he cried. "Wake up, Rabbit! We're going to put on a show!"

"But what could *I* do in a show?" asked Rabbit, rubbing her eyes.

"Bounce!" said Fletcher.

"You're the best bouncer in the woods!"

As news of the show spread,
the sleepy woods came to life,
filled with the sound of singing
and busy bouncing feet.

Squirrel went
hunting for sweet
wild strawberries.

The mice in
the meadow made
daisy chains.

Hedgehog
gathered pricklefuls
of velvety petals ...

... and Fletcher fetched
honeysuckle to decorate
the stage.

As day began to fade, the animals gathered,
murmuring excitedly, ready to watch the show.

When at last the crowd became silent, nightingales began
to sing, moth wings flickered, and the cricket band played.
Glowworms cast their gentle light onto the stage, and ...

... out bounced Rabbit,
glowing pink with pride.
   She flipped and flopped,
hopped and tumbled all around the stage.
   The more the crowd cheered,
the higher Rabbit leapt, until with
a triumphant twirl ...

... she waved for her friends to join her.

Then Squirrel juggled, the mice skipped,
the frogs croaked, and Hedgehog rolled, as
the sun set in a fiery golden blaze.

When the last act took their bow,
the animals clapped ...

... and called Fletcher onto the stage.

Fletcher looked out over the sea of smiling faces.
"Oh no," he gulped, "I've been so busy, I haven't planned anything."
"But you have," cried his friends. "You've planned ...

... this magical
musical night!"
The cricket band began to play again,
and the animals began to dance,
as the first stars sparkled brightly
in the darkening sky.